APR - - 2023

NO LONGER PROPERTY
SEATTLE PUBLIC LIBRARY

P9-AGA-280

© for the original edition: 2022 Verlagshaus
Jacoby & Stuart GmbH, Berlin, Germany
© text and illustrations: Britta Teckentrup
© for the English edition: 2022, Prestel Verlag,
Munich · London · New York
A member of Penguin Random House
Verlagsgruppe GmbH
Neumarkter Strasse 28 · 81673 Munich

Library of Congress Control Number: 2021948259
A CIP catalogue record for this book is available
from the British Library.

Translated from the German by Nicola Stuart.

Copy editing: Ayesha Wadhawan
Production management and typesetting:
Susanne Hermann
Printing and binding: TBB, a.s.

Prestel Publishing compensates the
CO$_2$ emissions produced from the making
of this book by supporting a reforestation
project in Brazil.
Find further information on the project here:
www.ClimatePartner.com/14044-1912-1001

MIX
From responsible sources
FSC® C022120

FSC
www.fsc.org

Our production is
climate neutral
ClimatePartner.com/14044-1912-1001
Print product

Penguin Random House Verlagsgruppe
FSC® N001967

Printed in Slovakia

ISBN 978-3-7913-7519-9
www.prestel.com

Britta Teckentrup

Big Hedgehog and Little Hedgehog

Take an Evening Stroll

PRESTEL

Munich · London · New York

It was getting late. Big Hedgehog and Little Hedgehog were on their way home. The sun was low in the evening sky, and its last rays shone through the leaves.

"Wait a minute, Big Hedgehog!" called Little Hedgehog.

Big Hedgehog stopped and turned around.
"Can we wait together for the sun to set?"
asked Little Hedgehog.
They sat down side by side on the grass
and waited. They waited until the sun had
completely disappeared.

"We have to move on. It's getting late,
Little Hedgehog," said Big Hedgehog.

They went a little further until Little Hedgehog
called out again. "Wait a minute, Big Hedgehog!"
"And what are we waiting for now?"
asked Big Hedgehog smilingly.
"Now we're waiting for the moon to rise!"
replied Little Hedgehog, and grinned.
"Of course!" said Big Hedgehog.
And they waited together until the moon
had risen and begun its journey in the sky.

"It's late, Little Hedgehog," said Big Hedgehog.
"Let's go on."

As they walked on, they passed a field of beautiful flowers.
"Wait a minute, Big Hedgehog! Do you smell that too?"
Big Hedgehog stopped, and they both held their noses in the air.
"Those are wildflowers that smell so nice, Little Hedgehog."

And they stood there for a long time and inhaled the sweet scent of the flowers.

"But now, that's enough!" said Big Hedgehog.

They went on their way. After some time,
Little Hedgehog called out, "Wait a minute,
Big Hedgehog! Do you hear that too?"
Big Hedgehog stopped. They both were silent
and listened.
"Tu-whit, tu-whoo. Tu-whit, tu-whoo."
"Those must be the owls," said Big Hedgehog.
"Can we visit the owls together?" asked
Little Hedgehog.
Big Hedgehog and Little Hedgehog followed
the "tu-whit, tu-whoo" until they reached
the owls' tree. And they waved good night
at the owls from below.

"We must get going now, Little Hedgehog.
It's getting later and later," said Big Hedgehog.

Just as they were about to move on, a large
cloud covered the moon.
"Wait a minute, Big Hedgehog! Let's stop for
a moment until we can see the moon again."
And they looked up to the sky and waited until
the moon shone brightly again.

"Now it's *really* late, Little Hedgehog.
Come on, let's hurry," said Big Hedgehog,
and walked a little faster.

A bit further on, they passed a pond.

Little Hedgehog called out, "Big Hedgehog, wait a minute!

We still have to say good night to the fish and the frogs."

And they said good night to every fish and listened
to the frogs' evening song.
"It's getting cold, Little Hedgehog. Come now,
we're going home!" said Big Hedgehog.

But Little Hedgehog wasn't there anymore. A tiny firefly glittered and glowed in the night, and Little Hedgehog was following it further and further into the shrubs.

"Wait a minute, Little Hedgehog!" called Big Hedgehog.
"Where are you going?"

Big Hedgehog found Little Hedgehog
hidden in the deep grass of a meadow.
"Do you see the beautiful flying lights?"
Little Hedgehog asked with big eyes.
"These are called fireflies, Little Hedgehog,"
explained Big Hedgehog. "Wow. I don't
think I've ever seen a meadow so magical!"
And they forgot the time and watched
the fireflies dance.

After a long while, Big Hedgehog said,
"Now we *have* to go!"

They were almost home when Little Hedgehog
called out, "Please Big Hedgehog,
wait one more time!"
"Well, what is it now?" asked Big Hedgehog
with a smile.
Little Hedgehog looked at Big Hedgehog
with sleepy eyes and said, yawning,
"Let's count the stars!"
And so they sat down and counted the stars,
one at a time, until they ran out of numbers.

"Let's go on, Little Hedgehog. We're almost home,"
whispered Big Hedgehog gently...

...but Little Hedgehog
had already fallen asleep.